The HUEYs in

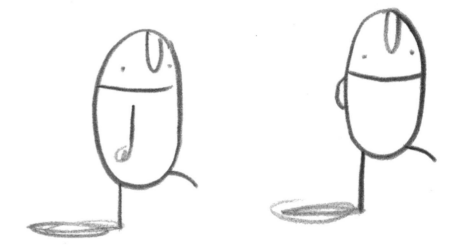

To Tommy, grandfather of all Hueys

First published in hardback by HarperCollins Children's Books in 2012
First published in paperback in 2012

10 9 8 7 6

ISBN: 978-0-00-742066-7

HarperCollins Children's Books is a division of HarperCollins Publishers Ltd.

Visit our website at: www.harpercollins.co.uk

Printed and bound in China

The HUEYS in THE NEW JUMPER

bla bla blabity bla

mm hmm

OLIVER JEFFERS

HarperCollins *Children's Books*

The thing about the Hueys...

...was that they were all the same.

There were many, many of them...

...and they
all looked
the same,

thought
the
same...

and

did

the

same

things…

…until the day one of them
– Rupert was his name –
knitted a nice new jumper.

He wore it all over the place,
proud as could be.

Not everyone agreed with his taste though...

Rupert went to Gillespie.

Gillespie thought being different
was interesting.

He decided to knit
himself a nice new
jumper to match.

YAY!

That way,
he would be
different too!

When the other Hueys saw Gillespie beside him, they didn't think that Rupert was so strange any more.

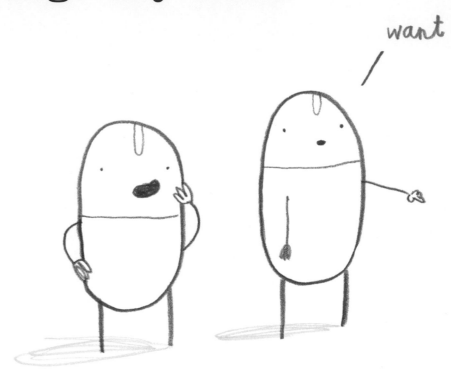

Being different was catching on…

...and they
wanted
to be
different
too!

One by one, new jumpers started popping up everywhere.

Before long, they were
all different, and no one
was the same any more.

**Then Rupert decided
he liked the idea of
wearing a hat.**

And that changed everything...

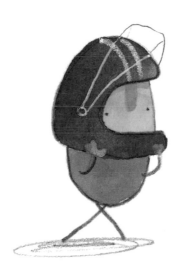

Have you read these brilliant picture books by OLIVER JEFFERS?

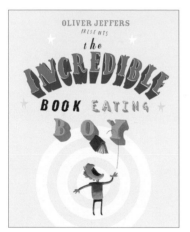

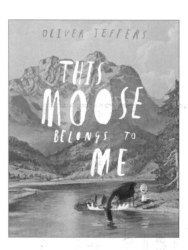

And look out for The HUEYS in IT WAS NOT ME